Franky

Meri Murphy and Tsalaph Murphy Koerner

Meri Murphy   *Tsalaph M.K.*

PAGE PUBLISHING, INC.
New York, NY

First originally published by Page Publishing, Inc. 2018

ISBN 978-1-64082-249-8 (Paperback)
ISBN 978-1-64082-250-4 (Digital)

Printed in the United States of America

This is Franky. Franky is an adventurous ladybug who loves to fly. Franky is not like any other ladybug with spots on his back. He has only one spot on his back, and it is the shape of a heart.

One cold morning, Franky looks way up, up in the sky, and wonders how high he can fly. He looks around and spots a GIGANTIC windmill.

Franky wants to fly up to the windmill, but he knows it is really far, and he will have to take a few breaks along the way.

Franky sees a BIG yellow flower nearby. He flies to the tippy-top of the flower. "Whew! That was far!" Franky is sleepy; he yawns and falls asleep.

Unexpectedly, Franky wakes up to a loud *bzzzz* sound. A grumpy bumblebee has landed on the flower!

Franky is frightened, so he quickly flies away!

Franky is soon tired and needs a place to rest. He spots a large wooden bucket. He flies to the tippy-top of the bucket. "Oh my! That was far!"

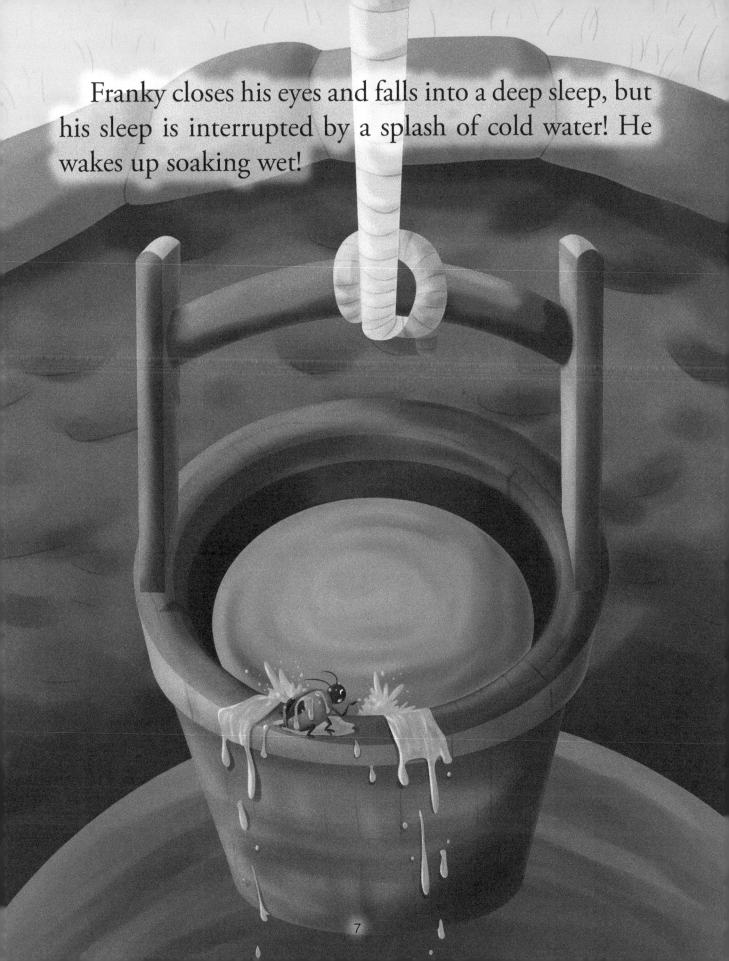

Franky closes his eyes and falls into a deep sleep, but his sleep is interrupted by a splash of cold water! He wakes up soaking wet!

Cold and startled, Franky quickly flies away!

Franky is weary. He spots a little pink nose nearby.

He flies to the tippy-top of the nose and really wants to take a nap, but suddenly two small hands try to grab Franky! He is scared, so he quickly flies away.

Franky is exhausted and really, really wants to sleep. He notices a tall scarecrow nearby. He flies to the tippy-top of the scarecrow. "Whoa! That was far!"

Franky decides to take a nap and is soon fast asleep, but his nap is disturbed by a huge black bird trying to snatch Franky in its beak!

Franky is terrified, so he quickly flies away.

Franky is worn out! He sees a brick chimney nearby. He flies to the tippy-top of the chimney. "Gee-whiz! That was far!"

Franky lies down and takes a nap, but it is a short nap, because suddenly black smoke begins billowing out of the chimney! There is smoke everywhere! Franky begins coughing and is very frightened, so he quickly flies away.

Franky is cold, scared, dirty, and tired.

But he looks up and sees that the windmill is so close. Franky opens his wings and begins to fly.

He finally makes it to the tippy-top of the windmill.

Franky looks down from the windmill to see how far he has come; he sees the brick chimney with the black smoke, the tall scarecrow with the huge black bird, the little pink nose with the two small hands, the large wooden bucket full of cold water, and the big yellow flower with the grumpy bumblebee. "Wow! What an adventure!"

Franky is proud of himself for making it such a long way. Now he can take a rest, a very long rest! Franky closes his eyes and falls fast asleep, dreaming of his exciting adventure.

About the Author

Meri Murphy is a children's book author who currently lives in Northern Colorado with her husband and three amazing children. Meri has the privilege and adventure of being a mother and an aunt, both of which have offered her a front row seat to children's wonder and creativity. Her stories are infused with personal experiences and from the fabrications of the ever curious minds of her nieces, nephews and her own children.

Tsalaph Murphy Koerner has had a love for reading and writing her whole life. Tsalaph has been writing children's books for the last several years, her inspiration and passion comes from her love of reading with her children. She and her husband currently live in Western Montana with their four beautiful boys.

CPSIA information can be obtained
at www.ICGtesting.com
Printed in the USA
JSHW020838031119
2216JS00001B/10

9 781640 822498